Tyrannosaurus rex

Parasaurolophus

Stegosaurus

Diplodocus

Suchomimus

Compsognathus

Triceratops

Pachycephalosaurus

Pterodactyl

Plateosaurus

Ankylosaurus

Sinosauropteryx

Allosaurus

Velociraptor

Iguanodon

Archaeopteryx

Brontosaurus

Oviraptor

To Macey-Jayne,
sweet dreams always – M.S.

To KN for all his
support and
friendship – T.B.

This Dover edition, first published in 2023,
is an unabridged republication of the work published by Scholastic
Children's Books, a division of Scholastic Ltd., London, in 2021.
The text has been modified for this US edition.

International Standard Book Number

ISBN-13: 978-0-486-85188-4
ISBN-10: 0-486-85188-5

Printed in China by C & C Offset Printing Co., Ltd.
85188501   2023
www.doverpublications.com

MARK SPERRING   TIM BUDGEN

20 DINOSAURS at BEDTIME

DOVER PUBLICATIONS
Garden City, New York

Once upon a bedtime, these children could not sleep.

ROAR!

So their helpful moms and daddies said that they should count some sheep.

Though children think
that sheep are nice,
there's something
they like more.

So, instead of counting
lots of sheep,
they counted . . .

Dinosaurs!

1...

Here's a dinosaur
who's been awake all day.

2...

Here's a dinosaur
who wants to
roll and play.

3...

Here's a dinosaur
splashing
through the mud.

4...
Here's a
dinosaur
whose
giant feet go

THUD!

5...

Here's a dinosaur chasing its own tail.

6...

Here's a dinosaur...

who's **slightly** scared of snails!

7...

Here's a dinosaur
watching the sun set.

8...

Here's a dinosaur

who isn't tired yet.

9...
Here's a dinosaur who's counting fireflies.

10...
Here's a dinosaur with very sleepy eyes.

11...

Here's a dinosaur whose wings are tucked up tight.

12...

Here's a dinosaur who's whispering, "Goodnight!"

Yes, once upon a bedtime,

while counting
dinosaurs,

this bedtime bunch
snuggled down

and snored loud,
sleepy snores.

But in their dreams
they kept on counting
dinosaurs they met . . .

13...

14...

15...

And they're not done counting yet!

16...

Here's a dinosaur who
made a squeak then
hatched!

18...

Here's a dinosaur
in a leafy nest.

19...

Here's a dinosaur who
knows it's time to rest.

20!

Here's a dinosaur–
the last one that they found.

It gave them all a playful nudge,
then scooped them off the ground.

They walked through starlit forests,
beneath the moon's soft light.

Once upon a bedtime,
on a count-to-twenty night!

10

16

11

12

13

17

18

14

19

15

20